D1301962

What Kids Say About
Carole Marsh Mysteries . . .

I love the real locations! Reading the book always makes me want to go and visit them all on our next family vacation. My Mom says maybe, but I can't wait!

One day, I want to be a real kid in one of Ms. Marsh's mystery books. I think it would be fun, and I think I am a real character anyway. I filled out the application and sent it in. I hope they pick me!

History was not my favorite subject till I started reading Carole Marsh Mysteries. Ms. Marsh really brings history to life. Also, she leaves room for the scary and fun.

I think the characters are so smart and brave. They are lucky because they get to do so much cool stuff! I always wish I could be right there with them!

The kids in the story are cool and funny! They make me laugh a lot! I like that there are boys and girls in the story of different ages. Some mysteries I outgrow, but I can always find a favorite character to identify with in these books.

They are scary, but not too scary. They are funny. I learn a lot. There is always food, which makes me hungry. I feel like I am there.

What Parents and Teachers Say About Carole Marsh Mysteries . . .

I think kids love these books because they have such a wealth of detail. I know I learn a lot reading them! It's an engaging way to look at the history of any place or event. I always say I'm only going to read one chapter to the kids, but that never happens—it's always two or three, at least!
—Librarian

Reading the mystery and going on the field trip—Scavenger Hunt in hand—was the most fun our class ever had! It really brought the place and its history to life. They loved the real kids characters and all the humor. I loved seeing them learn that reading is an experience to enjoy!
—4th grade teacher

Carole Marsh is really on to something with these unique mysteries. They are so clever; kids want to read them all. The Teacher's Guides are chock full of activities, recipes, and additional fascinating information. My kids thought I was an expert on the subject—and with this tool, I felt like it!
—3rd grade teacher

My students loved writing their own mystery book! Ms. Marsh's reproducible guidelines are a real jewel. They learned about copyright and more & ended up with their own book they were so proud of!
—Reading/Writing Teacher

"The kids seem very realistic—my children seemed to relate to the characters. Also, it is educational by expanding their knowledge about the famous places in the books."

"They are what children like: mysteries and adventures with children they can relate to."

"Encourages reading for pleasure."

"This series is great. It can be used for reluctant readers, and as a history supplement."

Dear Pirate:

The
Buried
Treasure
Mystery

By Carole Marsh

Published by Gallopade International/Carole Marsh Books. Printed
in the United States of America.

Managing Editor: Sherry Moss
Senior Editor: Janice Baker
Assistant Editor: Beverly Melasi
Cover Design: Vicki DeJoy
Illustrations: Yvonne Ford

Gallopade International is introducing SAT words that kids need to
know in each new book tht we publish. The SAT words are bold in the
story. Look for this special logo **SAT** beside each word.

Gallopade is proud to be a member and supporter of these
educational organizations and associations:

American Booksellers Association
American Library Association
International Reading Association
National Association for Gifted Children
The National School Supply and Equipment Association
The National Council for the Social Studies
Museum Store Association
Association of Partners for Public Lands

20 Years Ago . . .

As a mother and an author, one of the fondest periods of my life was when I decided to write mystery books for children. At this time (1979) kids were pretty much glued to the TV, something parents and teachers complained about the way they do about web surfing and blogging today.

I decided to set each mystery in a real place—a place kids could go and visit for themselves after reading the book. And I also used real children as characters. Usually a couple of my own children served as characters, and I had no trouble recruiting kids from the book's location to also be characters.

Also, I wanted all the kids—boys and girls of all ages—to participate in solving the mystery. And, I wanted kids to learn something as they read. Something about the history of the location. And I wanted the stories to be funny. That formula of real+scary+smart+fun served me well.

I love getting letters from teachers and parents who say they read the book with their class or child, then visited the historic site and saw all the places in the mystery for themselves. What's so great about that? What's great is that you and your children have an experience that bonds you together forever. Something you shared. Something you both cared about at the time. Something that crossed all age levels—a good story, a good scare, a good laugh!

20 years later,
Carole Marsh

Christina "Mystery Girl" Mimi Papa Grant

Hey, kids! As you see, here we are ready to embark on another of our exciting Carole Marsh Mystery adventures. My grandchildren often travel with me all over the world as I research new books. We have a great time together, and learn things we will carry with us for the rest of our lives!

I hope you will go to www.carolemarshmysteries.com and explore the many Carole Marsh Mysteries series!

Well, the Mystery Girl is all tuned up and ready for "take-off!" Gotta go...Papa says so! Wonder what I've forgotten this time?

Happy "Armchair Travel" Reading,

Mimi

P.S. Send _me_ a postcard ... and receive a postcard from a ... **Pirate!**

About the Characters

Paul Post is the postmaster of the post office in Postcard, Pennsylvania. He's quiet, soft-spoken and a bit of a worrywart. He's not a whiz at electronics, but can hold his own. He hates to drive, and doesn't always like to be the one in charge.

Penelope Post is a street-smart, independent mother with her own postcard company. She doesn't know much about technology, and likes to run around in curlers and sweat clothes. She loves homeschooling her children and taking trips, because every trip is an education you can't get in books.

Peter Post inherited his mother's love for traveling. He's an 11-year old who loves to figure out puzzles, riddles, and a good mystery, of course. Peter never goes anywhere without his backpack, which contains his laptop and spy paraphernalia.

Piper Post inherited her mother's sassiness. She's a very smart 10-year-old, but doesn't like school very much. Piper loves her adventures with her brother and usually uncovers the last bit of information to help Peter solve the mystery. She also loves to tell knock-knock jokes, just to annoy Peter!

Books in This Series

Table of Contents

Travel with the
Post Family:

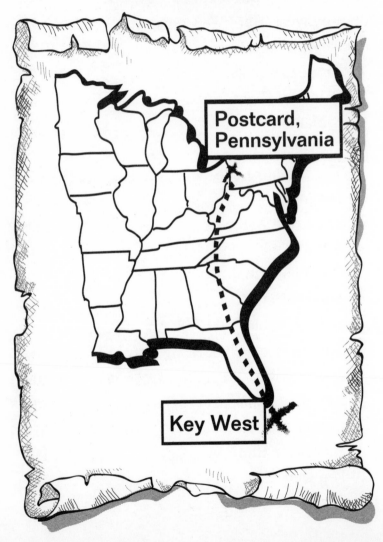

Postcard,
Pennsylvania

Key West

Prologue

Peter was restless. It was almost dawn before he actually slept soundly. He dreamed of howling winds and the blast of cannons off in the distance. Cannons? And there was someone talking to him through it all...someone whispering, saying something he couldn't hear because of the whistling wind. But as he listened desperately, he was sure that the voice was his sister's and she was saying, "PIRATES!"

Peter strained against the scratchy, thick ropes that held him fast against an old wooden chair. Brother and sister were tied back to back so he couldn't see her, but Peter could feel the strain against his chest whenever Piper moved. He spat out the dirty rag someone had used as a gag, but he didn't dare speak to Piper, for fear that she'd call out. He didn't want to alert their captors.

Peter looked nervously toward the door where he could hear them laughing. The ship suddenly dipped, causing the door to crack open far enough so he could see the pirates. One had several gleaming

gold teeth, and the other wore a patch over his left eye.

"Arrr, the treasure be ours now, Cap'n. Should we get rid of the boy and the wench?" the pirate with the eyepatch asked.

"Aye, Mr. Downey," the pirate with the gold teeth answered. "I say we make 'em walk the plank!"

Peter heard Piper whimper against her gag. He needed to rid himself of the ropes quickly, so he could free Piper, too. He played with the intricate knots in the ropes. Sailor knots, Peter thought. Boy, someone sure knew what they were doing when they tied these. He had to hurry. Piper was waiting for him to rescue her.

"Peter!" Piper cried his name through her gag.

"Huh?' Peter whispered sleepily.

"Hurry up, Peter, or you'll be late for breakfast!" Piper yelled as she shook his leg.

Peter's eyes popped open. He wanted to ask Piper how she'd managed to escape the pirates, but all he saw was the back of her pajamas as she sprinted out of his bedroom.

Prologue

He wiped his hands down his face. "I've got to stop eating chocolate chip cookies before bed," he said with a chuckle.

"They give me such baaaaaad....

dreams!"

A Puzzling Pirate

"Is it Friday yet?" 11-year-old Peter Post asked as he rushed into the cheerful kitchen, tossing his backpack on the table.

His mom, Penelope Post, was busy whisking eggs in a bright yellow bowl. One of the curlers that seemed to be part of her daily wardrobe had unraveled itself and was dangling just below her ear. "Why, do you have a big day planned today?" she asked jokingly.

Peter's 10-year-old sister, Piper, was already at the table pouring cereal. "Mom's wearing her blue sponge curlers today, silly," she remarked. "Of course it's Friday."

"Oh, yeah, I forgot." Peter grabbed the milk carton from the fridge, sloshed it over his cereal, and sat down to eat. "Dad said the pen pal postcards would be in today, and I don't want to miss out!"

Mom chuckled and patted a few stray black hairs back into their curler. "We're going to meet everyone at the post office at noon," she said with a smile. "How does that sound to you?"

"Fine," Peter garbled through a mouthful of cereal. He wanted to hurry.

Piper leaned her head on her hand, as she watched her brother inhale his breakfast amidst a sea of cereal boxes on the table. "Gee whiz, take a breath already," she said.

Peter stuck out his tongue and showed Piper a mouthful of half-chewed cereal.

"Mom!" Piper cried.

"Mom!" Peter mocked.

Mom waved her wooden spoon at them. "Enough, both of you! Let's hurry and eat so we can be on time."

Peter rubbed his hands together. "This is going to be a fun day," he said, his eyes twinkling. "I hope there'll be a whole lot of postcards to pick through!"

Within the hour, the Post family was on their way. The kids' excitement made their mom smile. The postcard pen pal club had been her idea. While visiting the post office a few weeks ago to mail designer postcards from her home-based Internet company, she had run into some local women who also home-schooled their children. They were looking for a new project to interest their kids over the summer. So, she presented the idea to them over coffee at the local café.

And the rest is history, Mom thought, as she backed her SUV into a shady parking space under a huge oak tree. Postcard, Pennsylvania often got very warm in the summer. She gave her horn a quick toot and jumped out to open the hatch. Her husband, Paul Post, the town's postmaster, personally wheeled a large mail cart out to help her unload.

In a flash, the van's side doors flew open. The kids dashed past him with a quick, "Hi, Dad!" and raced through the automatic double doors.

Several children were already there waiting. Mr. Post carried in a large basket filled with postcards. The children's eyes opened wide. They all chanted.

"Oooo, ahhhh!"

"There must be hundreds of them!" Peter squealed. "I'm sure to find the right pen pal!"

A Puzzling Pirate

Mr. Post looked anxious as the group of boys and girls revved up like small panthers ready to pounce. He feared for his clean, orderly post office, so he up held his hands in defense. "Let's keep this as organized as we can, okay?" he said. He dumped the basket on the large work table, and the children cheered. "Hooray!!"

Peter got right to it. He grabbed a handful of postcards and began to sift through them. He looked at the first one. "No." Then the second. "No." Pretty soon he was shuffling through them like a deck of cards. "No...no...no."

Finally, one card caught his eye. It was a bright red postcard with FLORIDA printed across it. "Florida, wow!" Peter could hardly wait to see who sent it. His mouth fell open

when he turned it over.

"Oh, my gosh! Oh, my gosh!" he cried.

Mom caught the astonished look on his face as he read the back of the card. "What is it, Peter?" she asked. His excitement was **contagious**. "Who's the postcard from? Someone famous?"

He looked up and smiled. "It's from...it's from... *A PIRATE!*"

Return to Sender

Avast, Ye Land Lubber!

Me parrot and I'd like to
say, "Shiver me timbers!"
but it's much too warm
here for that so we'll
just say, "Ahoy Matey!"

Yer friend, Captain Kid
P. O. Box 103
Key West, FL 33040

Home School
Pen Pal Club
P.O. Box 5
Postcard, PA 00123

Peter's mom looked stunned. "Pirate, as in 'Arrrr'?"

Peter saluted her. "Aye, aye, matey!"

"Let me see that," Mom demanded. Peter handed over the postcard, and she frowned. "This must be some kind of joke. Children are not pirates!" She flipped the card over a few times. "Is there a return address?"

Peter pointed to the post office box listed on the card. He was amazed. First, he had dreamed of pirates, and now he got a mysterious postcard from one. "I want to write him back. Can I write him back, Mom, pleeeeeeease?" he pleaded.

Mom's eyebrows drew together in concern as she looked at her husband. "What do you think, dear?"

Mr. Post looked down into Peter's twinkling blue eyes, and already knew his answer. If something as simple as a postcard could put such happiness on his son's face, who was he to

disappoint him? He laid his hands on Peter's shoulders. "I don't see what harm it could do," he said. "Go ahead and let the boy write this Captain Kid back and see what happens."

"Dad, you are so totally awesome!" Peter shouted, and gave his dad a high-five.

Peter sat down after dinner to write his new friend. He knew a little about pirates from movies. This could turn out to be a big hoax and he'd end up looking silly, he thought. But what if it really was an honest-to-goodness, swash-buckling, yo-ho-ho and all-that-stuff pirate? That thought alone inspired him to pick up his pen. He took a deep breath. "Oh well, here goes!"

Yo-ho-ho, Captain Kid,

Are you really a pirate?
I don't know much
pirate talk. Hey, maybe
you can teach me!
My sister Piper is 10,
and I'm 11. We live in
Postcard, Pennsylvania.

Yer friend,
Peter

Captain Kid
P.O. Box 103
Key West, FL 33040

Early the next morning, Peter hurried to
catch his dad before he left for the post office.
He could hear him in the foyer by the door.
"Hey, Dad," Peter said. He held the postcard
nervously behind his back and rocked on both

heels. "Uhh, will you mail something for me today?"

Mr. Post saw the **anxiety** on his son's face. "Sure," he said, adjusting the official post office cap that was part of his uniform. "Whatcha got?"

Peter blushed as he handed over the postcard.

Dad looked solemnly at the address. "Are you sure you want to do this, son?" he asked. "It may be just be a prank."

Peter's enthusiasm showed on his face. "Yeah, but what if it isn't?" He grabbed his dad's arm and held on tight. "Just think, a real live pirate living somewhere in Florida!"

Piper entered the foyer and saw Peter hand over the postcard. "You're not really going to answer that, are you?" she asked. At his slight nod, she held her hand to her mouth and giggled. "Wait'll I tell my new pen pal, Samantha, that my brother is writing to some would-be pirate. What a hoot!"

"Now see here, wench..." Peter said, clenching his teeth. Hey, I said a pirate word, Peter thought. Where did that come from?

"Peter!" Mom yelled from the kitchen. "Apologize to your sister this instant!"

Peter and his dad were stunned. "That woman can hear through walls," Dad said, trying to look stern. "Go ahead, Peter, say you're sorry."

Piper crossed her arms over her chest. "Yes, Peter, I'm waiting," she said, anxiously tapping her toe.

Peter gently tugged at one of Piper's dark brown pigtails. "I'm sorry, wench," he said.

Dad tried to hide a smile. He playfully ruffled Peter's hair as he pushed the screen door open and skipped down the steps, singing softly. Peter was almost sure he heard, "Yo-ho-ho, and a bottle of rum..."

A few days later, Dad came home from work, waving a postcard. Peter gazed at the colorful picture of a Florida sunset in Key West.

"It's from him!"

Peter shouted. He quickly turned it over. The ink on the postcard was smeared a little, like rain had splattered on it. Peter ran his hand over it, and imagined that maybe there had been a hurricane where the pirate was living in Key West. Peter knew that Florida was often battered by hurricanes in the summer and fall.

Peter read the message out loud.

Ahoy, me Buckos!

I'm truly a pirate, that I be. I sail me ship upon the sea. I stay up late, till half past three. And there's a peg below me knee. If ye both be willin' ta weather the tide, come and see me anytime!

Yer friend, Captain Kid

Home School
Pen Pal Club
P.O. Box 5
Postcard, PA 00123

"He wants us to come and see him!" Peter shouted. "Can we, Dad? Can we?"

Dad rubbed his chin. "Well, it just so happens I got a postcard myself today from an old Navy buddy of mine who lives in Key West. He's invited all of us to go deep sea fishing next week."

"WHOOO HOOO!!"

Peter shouted. "It's perfect!" He jumped up and down, pumping his fists wildly in the air. "Wait till I tell Piper!"

"Hold on there, Matey," Dad said, as he gently pulled Peter back by his collar. "I have to talk this over with your mother first. She's not real fond of boats, you know."

"But you'll try, right?" Peter asked hopefully.

Dad patted his head. "Yes, Peter, I'll try," he replied. "You wouldn't want to disappoint a pirate—that could be hazardous to your health!"

22

2

Key West, Here We Come!

Later that evening, the Post parents called a family meeting in the dining room. When both children were seated on the couch, their dad began. "We've decided to take a trip to Key West next Friday," he announced. "Your mother and I feel it can be an important educational experience for both of you."

Peter blinked hard. The delivery of that speech was definitely their dad, but the words coming out of his mouth were undeniably their mom's. Peter smiled to himself. How did parents do that?

Peter and Piper immediately wrote a postcard to their new pirate friend. Piper came up with lots of pirate lingo.

Avast, Captain Kid!

Me sis still thinks ye just might be pullin' our leg about being a pirate. Arrr! We're going to be in Key West next weekend! We can hook up with ye then if ye a mind ta.

Yer friends,
Peter & Piper

Captain Kid
P.O. Box 103
Key West, FL 33040

The next morning, Mom issued an assignment at the breakfast table.

"Avast me hearties, yo-ho! I've a task for ye."

She laid typed sheets of paper on the table in front of them. "Here be copies of pirate vocabulary words and their definitions. It be yer task to match 'em up." She wiggled her eyebrows. "We be review'n 'em together later tonight." And with that, she saluted them, whirled on her heels, and left the room.

It was hard work. At least three or four of the pirate words could match up with several definitions. Mom checked in on them just before noon and was surprised at what little progress they had made. "If ye be gettin' a little more work done, I might be feedin' ye some grub. If not, ye'll be walkin' the plank!"

Peter stole a glance in his sister's direction. "Me thinks her curlers are wrapped too tight," he said.

By mid-afternoon, the kids had gotten into the spirit of things and were having fun. They spoke pirate lingo to their mom and each other for the rest of the day. Peter was sure he and his sister could communicate more clearly now with their new friend. Well, he'd wait and see if he got another card.

Sure enough, it came two days later!

Yo-ho, me friends,

I have a tale of treasure, plunder, sea and sail. One man's loss was another man's gain. The eye of a storm caused the ship to wane.

Can't wait to see ye, so don't be late. Look to the keys for pieces of eight!

Yer friend, Captain Kid

Home School
Pen Pal Club
P.O. Box 5
Postcard, PA 00123

"He's trying to tell us something!" Peter exclaimed. He winked at Piper. "Me thinks, there be a mystery afloat here, little wench," he said.

"Me thinks I smell trouble afloat," Piper groaned.

Peter wiggled his eyebrows at her. "Not me, I smell treasure!"

"Oh, great! Here we go again." Piper threw her hands in the air. "Just how does one smell treasure?"

Her brother grinned. "By standin' near the poop deck, of course!"

The next morning, Piper helped Peter pack his backpack with all his detective gear. He never left home without it. When they raced

downstairs with their suitcases, their parents were already loading the SUV.

Huffing and puffing, Peter raced to the mailbox and tossed in the last postcard with their itinerary written on it.

Yo Captain Kid,

Here's our itinerary:
Parrot Head Hotel
Mallory Square
Southernmost tip
Downtown Key West

Your friends,
Peter & Piper

Captain Kid
P.O. Box 103
Key West, FL 33040

He raised the flag on the mailbox, then stooped over, trying to catch his breath.

"Hey, you okay?" Piper ran up the driveway and patted Peter on the back. "Pirate woman over there says to get the lead out!"

Mom was busy barking orders like a true pirate captain. "Avast ye swabbies! Weigh anchor! Raise the main sail! In other words, let's get this show on the road!"

3
Ahoy, Mateys!

The Post family SUV crossed one small key, or island, after another until finally reaching Key West late in the afternoon. Scooters whizzed past, and people roamed the shops everywhere. Key West had the tropical atmosphere of the Caribbean Islands. Festive music filled the air, and most of the tourists wore colorful beads around their necks.

"There's our hotel on the right, dear," Mom pointed. They pulled into the Parrot Head Hotel

parking lot and a man wearing a pirate costume stepped up to help them with their luggage. "Ahoy, Mateys! Yer just in time ta watch the sunset!" He smiled, and his gold teeth gleamed in the sunlight.

Peter and Piper jumped out of the car and ran past him into the hotel. The lobby was brightly painted in pink and green hues and was decorated with historical Key West photographs.

"aHOY!"

Peter said to the pirate behind the tall, polished registration desk.

32

"aHOY, YeRSeLF!"

he answered. "Me name's Captain Seaweed." He swept off his pirate hat. "And who might ye be?" he asked, leaning forward low enough to be eye level with Peter and Piper. His eyepatch made him look positively wicked.

There was something vaguely familiar about him, and Peter tried to shake off the strange feeling that they'd met before. "I'm Peter Post and this is my sister, Piper. Do you, by any chance, have a postcard for us?" he asked.

The pirate turned to the mail slots. "As a matter of fact, I do," he remarked with a sly smile. He handed Peter a postcard with a colorful Macaw parrot on the front.

Ahoy, me Buckos!

I like to fish, I like to fight. I like to stay up half the night.

When I say "starboard," ye go right. Me ma, she says, ye'll like the sights.

Yer friend, Captain Kid

Home School
Pen Pal Club
P.O. Box 5
Postcard, PA 00123

"Oh boy, it's from him!"

Peter exclaimed. He and Piper couldn't wait for
their adventure to begin!

36

4
Pirates and Psychics

The Post family took to the streets following the pirates' instructions. They blended right in with the masses of people, both locals and tourists, who had flocked to the water's edge at Mallory Square to watch the sunset.

Excitement and anticipation filled the air as the sun sank into the Gulf of Mexico. Immediately, the clouds were lit with a reddish-purple and golden glow. Peter thought how

great it would be to live the life of a pirate and be able to see a spectacular sunset like that every evening.

Once darkness fell, entertainers including jugglers, tightrope walkers, and fire-eaters thrilled the crowds.

Suddenly, a voice boomed over a loudspeaker, announcing the main event. "Ladies and gentlemen! Welcome to Pirates of the Caribbean!" the voice bellowed, and the show began. "Many years ago, ruthless men ravaged the ships of the Caribbean and captured innocent passengers, turning them into pirates!"

The kids' eyes lit up. "Can we stay awhile and watch, Mom?" Peter asked.

Mom glanced around at the crowd. It looked safe enough. "Okay, but don't wander off," she warned. "Your dad and I will be looking at the silver jewelry on display right over there," she said, pointing to a nearby stand.

The frightening pirates came into view. One pirate had long black hair tied back with a colorful bandana, and a large gold earring that

sparkled in the spotlight. "I be Cap'n Slappy, and I be needin' some victims."

He spoke to the crowd, but looked directly at Peter and Piper. "Arrr, ye be just the right size, swabbies!" Everyone howled with laughter as he led them on stage. His weather-worn face curved into a crooked smile that highlighted gleaming gold teeth. He whispered to Peter, "So we meet again, eh, matey?"

Peter paled. That face! He was sure

he'd seen this pirate before, but how was that possible?

The pirate motioned for the kids to sit on some old wooden chairs. He started to tie Peter and Piper back to back. Alarm bells went off in Peter's head. Was this déjà vu all over again?

Another pirate joined them on stage. "Arrr, the treasure be ours now, Cap'n. Should we get rid of the boy and the wench?" the pirate with the eyepatch asked.

"Aye, Mr. Downey," the pirate with the gold teeth answered. "I say we make 'em walk the plank!"

Peter's head snapped up. Now he knew where he'd seen him before. In his dream! And the pirate with the eyepatch looked just like the manager of their hotel. But that couldn't be, could it? This was too weird!

Once the ropes were secured, the two pirates launched into mock battle with some other pirates. Swords clanged, and steel gleamed in the moonlight.

40

With a flick of his wrist, Cap'n Slappy cut the ropes between the two kids in one swoop. The crowd cheered and the show was over.

Peter practically leaped off the stage. He wanted to get as far away from Cap'n Slappy as he could! He hurried his sister toward the exit.

"Wait!" Cap'n Slappy said, running after them. He raised his sword as if ready to strike, and Peter flinched. Instead, he removed something from the tip. "Take this with ye." He handed Piper a postcard. When she turned it over, she and Peter were astonished to see that it was from their pirate pen pal.

Return to Sender

Ahoy, me Swabbies!

There once lived a
captain named **Mel**.
Who searched buried
treasure for a spell.
He fought for the gold
Until he was old
And lived high in **society**
as a **maritime** host.

Yer friend, Captain Kid

Home School
Pen Pal Club
P.O. Box 5
Postcard, PA 00123

Pirates and Psychics

The kids wanted to ask Cap'n Slappy how he knew about their pirate pen pal, but when they looked for him, he was gone.

"Well, what do you think of that?" Piper asked her brother.

"I think it was really weird, that's what I think," Peter said. He didn't want to tell Piper about his dream. Some things were just better left unsaid.

They checked in with their parents, who were still jewelry hunting. Peter noticed another booth nearby. "Look, that guy over there is reading a crystal ball," he said to Piper. They wandered over to watch. The sign read:

THE SPARROW SPEAKS OF FUTURE THINGS

46

Upon closer inspection, the kids could see that the crystal ball was shaped like a human skull! "Hey, maybe he can help us," Peter suggested. They huddled together and approached the fortune-teller with caution.

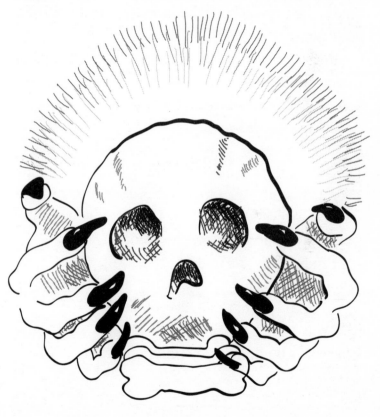

47

Piper was scared. "Mmm...maybe we should just wait for Mom and Dad," she said in a shaky voice.

Too late. He had spotted them. "Ah, children," he said, waving them over. "Come, come. Ze crystal ball, she is waiting to answer all your questions, yes?"

Piper immediately noticed was that his fingernails were long like claws, and painted black. She started to back up, but Peter stopped her. They sat down slowly.

The Sparrow tossed his shimmering black cape over his shoulders and waved his hands over the skull. Colored lights began to radiate from the crystal orb. "Ah, I see you've recently been on a long journey," he said.

Piper was stunned. "I...well, yes," she stammered. This was exciting and scary at the same time. "What else do you see?"

"You are looking for somezing, yes?" the Sparrow asked, his eyes fixed on Piper.

"Yes. Well, no," Piper stammered again. "Actually, we are looking for a person of sorts." The guy had her totally creeped out!

The Sparrow leaned forward, and this time stared into Peter's eyes. "The one you seek is near and has much to tell you about treasure, eh?" he said.

Peter's mouth dropped open. "How do you know this?" he asked.

"Why, Ze Sparrow, he knows all!" he stated. "But wait," he said, holding up a black lacquered fingernail. "He is not as he seems. He is...he is..." The Sparrow stopped.

"He's what?" Peter cried out. If something was wrong with their new friend, he wanted to help.

The Sparrow stared at the now dark skull. "There is nothing more to see," he said with a shrug.

"Peter, Piper!" The kids heard their mom calling. Piper was relieved. They were saved!

"Well," Piper said, pulling Peter along, "thank you, Mr. Sparrow, for sharing that

interesting information with us, but that's our mother calling. We have to go!"

"Wait! Ze Sparrow has something for you,"

he said, pulling a postcard from under his black top hat. The kids were again amazed as they read the words on the postcard.

Ahoy, me Mateys!

The key to me treasure
is near.
"X" marks the spot,
that is clear.
The white-headed man
will give ye my plan,
In a place that be filled
with great **heritage.**

Yer friend, Captain Kid

Home School
Pen Pal Club
P.O. Box 5
Postcard, PA 00123

Piper was a nervous wreck by the time they met up with their parents. She practically threw herself into her mom's arms.

"Well, did you two have a good time?" Mom asked.

Peter had the strangest feeling that they were being watched, but didn't want to say anything to upset his parents. He gave his sister "the look," and answered for both of them. "Yeah, sure. We had a great time!"

5
Pieces of Eight

The next morning, Dad went deep sea fishing with his friend. Peter and Piper didn't want to go. They were much more interested in trying to find their pirate pen pal. Mom said she'd "make the sacrifice" and stay with them all day.

They took to the road early to go sightseeing. While Mom drove, Peter told her about the pirates, Mr. Sparrow, and the postcards.

"Isn't that amazing?" he asked. "Mr. Sparrow was weird, though. You should have seen his long fingernails. I bet he could pick his nose all the way to his brain!" Peter said with a loud laugh.

"Peter!" his mom tried to sound stern, but she was giggling at the same time. "I think he upset your sister, though."

"Girls! Maybe we should go back and ask him some more questions," he teased.

Piper shuddered. "That guy was really creepy!"

"Whooooo..." Peter chanted and curled his hands into claws near Piper's face.

"Mom, Peter's trying to scare me again!" Piper whined.

"Cut it out, Peter and help me navigate," Mom said. "How far am I supposed to go on this road and which way do I turn?" They were headed for the famous Southernmost Point monument.

"Aren't you using the navigation system like Dad showed you before he left to go fishing?" Peter asked anxiously. "Mom, are we lost?"

She smiled at him in the rearview mirror. "Of course not, dear. We're on an adventure!"

Uh, oh. The kids knew whenever she said that, it always meant the same thing. "We're lost," they said in unison.

"Mom, the whole island is only four miles long, and two miles wide. How could you possibly be lost?" Piper whined.

"I told you I'm not lost. Hang on!" their mom shouted suddenly.

The SUV's tires squealed as Mom whipped it around a corner and came to a stop. "We're here," she said calmly. As Piper looked at her, stunned, Mom innocently tucked a stray hair back into her pink sponge roller.

Peter peeked out through the fingers he held over his eyes. "Did we die?"

"Of course not, silly," Mom laughed. She couldn't believe their luck finding a parking space so close. They walked across the street to the majestic monument. It was built to resemble a buoy.

"Look," Mom exclaimed, "it says that Cuba is only 90 miles away. I can't believe we're standing at the southernmost tip of the United States!"

BEEEEEEP!

BEEEEEEP!

BEEEEEEP!

A horn blared. Startled, Peter stared in the direction of the sound. A car waited to pass through the gate of the Southernmost House Hotel. An older gentleman hurried to let it through. When he tipped his hat at the guest, Peter noticed that he had white hair. Could it be that easy? He tugged on Piper's arm and pulled her along with him. As they approached, the gentleman waved at the children.

Peter felt silly. What if he was wrong? he thought. Well, there was no turning back now. He glanced at the man's name tag. "Excuse me, Mr. Joe," Peter said, looking nervous. "Do you by chance have a postcard for us?"

The white-haired man smiled and winked at them. "You betcha, sonny!" He felt in his bright red jacket, and then went to the inside pocket. He pulled out a brightly-colored postcard with a picture of the Atocha, a 16th century Spanish galleon that went down off the Keys in a hurricane.

Peter turned it over and read:

Ahoy, me Buckos!

There was a **museum**
of late.
That held many pieces
of eight.
He was a big wisher,
That Captain **Fisher**,
So the treasure
remained in this place.

Yer friend, Captain Kid

Home School
Pen Pal Club
P.O. Box 5
Postcard, PA 00123

Pieces of Eight

The kids turned to thank Mr. Joe, but he was gone. "Good grief, people come and go so quickly around here," Piper commented.

Dear Pirate: The Buried Treasure Mystery

6
X Marks the Spot!

Peter and Piper ran back over to their mom, still standing near the monument. "Hi, kids," she said cheerily. "Go stand next to the monument so I can take your picture." Piper gladly posed and made silly 10-year-old faces.

Peter wasn't interested in having his picture taken. He was thinking about all those postcards, and the fact that they were no closer

to finding their pirate now than they'd been back home. He slowly walked around the enormous monument, running his hand along its smooth surface. Suddenly, his hand caught on something taped to it. When he looked closely, he saw a piece of cardboard with an X painted on it.

"X marks the spot!" Peter yelled. Piper heard him shout and came running.

Peter removed the cardboard and turned it over. To his surprise, there was a postcard taped to it.

Return to Sender

Ahoy, me Mateys!

Silver bars were hard
ta land
From sunken treasure in
the sand.
Jewels be found in the
strangest places
Head to the beach,
then walk 40 paces.

Yer friend, Captain Kid

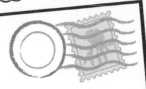

Home School
Pen Pal Club
P.O. Box 5
Postcard, PA 00123

X Marks the Spot!

As soon as they returned to their hotel, Mom said she was going to her room to get out of the sun. The kids begged to go to the beach across the street. "Okay, she agreed reluctantly. "I'll be watching you from the balcony, but be wary of strangers," she warned.

Peter felt kind of childish sifting sand into pails with the little pink shovels they'd purchased from a nearby gift shop. "Pretend we're making sand castles so we don't attract any attention," he whispered to Piper.

"Not attract any attention?" Piper blew the hair out of her eyes in frustration. "Peter Post, we've walked 40 paces in every direction possible and have practically dug up the whole beach! People will be falling in holes for days!"

The sky darkened and the wind picked up, causing the sand to blow. Piper stooped down to fill another bucket. "Would you mind telling me exactly what we're looking for?" she asked.

They were working now by the lamplight of a nearby shop. "I thought for sure we were going to find treasure," Peter muttered, suddenly feeling foolish.

As the sky grew darker, Peter stood and stretched his stiff legs. "Come on," he said, "let's go back to the hotel. This is a dead end."

X Marks the Spot!

Dear Pirate: The Buried Treasure Mystery

Treasure Trivia

Back in the hotel room, the light on the phone was flashing. The message from the front desk told the kids that they had mail. They raced downstairs to find a postcard with a picture of Old Town on it.

FIRST CLASS

Anchors Away, Buckos!

There once were some
pieces of eight
Ta see them ye go through
the gate.
Look to Duval
For a cannon and ball
So hurry, or ye'll be
too late!

Yer friend, Captain Kid

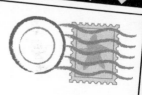

Home School
Pen Pal Club
P.O. Box 5
Postcard, PA 00123

INSUR

FRAGILE

"Another one," Peter said with a sigh. It was all beginning to annoy him. The pirate seemed to know exactly where they were, but they had no idea where he was. Peter sat at the table and laid all the cards out in front of him. The answer was here somewhere, of that he was sure. But where? He remembered his mom always told him to retrace his steps when he couldn't find something at home.

Maybe that's what he needed to do. Start over. Peter pulled out all the postcards and tried to reorganize them so they made more sense. He even took his magnifying glass out of his backpack to examine the pictures on the postcards for hidden clues. After an hour, he let out a loud sigh and threw them down.

Piper's voice broke the silence. "What are you doing?" she asked her brother.

Peter motioned to the scattered postcards. "I'm missing something," Peter said. "I need your help."

Piper shrugged. "What seems to be the problem?"

"I don't know exactly," he said, frowning. "Maybe I'm just taking us on a wild goose chase and I should stop trying."

Piper could see that Peter was really depressed over hitting a dead end. She decided to tease him and cheer him up. "I kind of want to get back to this whole thing about you asking me for help," she said. "Does that mean there's actually a mystery that 'Mr. All-Go,' 'No-Quit' Peter Post can't handle by himself and needs my advice?"

"Yeah, something like that," he grumbled.

Piper held up her hand.

"WHOA, WHOA, WHOA.

Is it something *like* that? Or is it *that*?" she teased.

Peter frowned. "Okay, it *is* that! Are you happy now? Girls...sheesh!"

Piper laughed. "Come on, let's get to work."

The kids examined the postcards again and again. Suddenly, Piper looked up. "Peter, did you notice that some of these words are highlighted?" Piper asked.

He looked at the cards again. Sure enough, some of the words were darker than the others. It was the missing piece! "Quick, hand me the cards," Peter ordered sharply. "We need to put these highlighted words together and see what they say!"

It was easier said than done.

They shuffled and reshuffled the postcards. They eliminated some, and rearranged the others again and again. Piper picked up the postcards and fanned them out in front of her. "I think we've got them in the right order this time. I can feel it!" she exclaimed.

When they put all the words together, it read:

MEL FISHER
MARITIME HERITAGE
SOCIETY MUSEUM

"We did it!" they shouted. Both kids jumped in the air and high-fived each other.

Peter stopped suddenly. "Hey, wait a minute," he said. "We forgot something."

"What?" Piper asked.

"We don't know where this place is located!" he groaned, pulling at his hair.

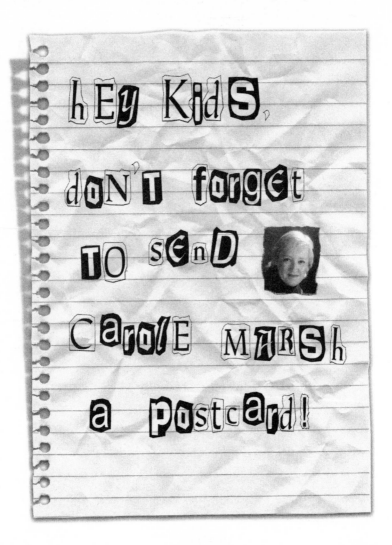

8
The Mother Lode!

The kids convinced their mom to take them to Old Town. It was late in the day, but some of the local stores were still open. Mom said she'd like to shop if the kids didn't mind walking around for a bit. It was the perfect opportunity for them to look for the museum.

They'd walked for a while when they came to a corner. Peter glanced at a signpost to see

where they were so they wouldn't get lost. They were on Duval Street.

"Quick, let me see those postcards!" he said. Piper dug them out of his backpack. "Oh, my gosh!" Peter shouted. "The museum is on Duval Street!"

Dark clouds hovered overhead, making it seem more like night than day. The first spattering of rain clanged on the metal roofs. Within minutes, they were under siege. Lightning flashed and thunder crashed!

"Peter, it's getting worse and I don't know where Mom is!" Piper shouted above the raging storm.

DUVAL STREET

The Mother Lode!

Peter grabbed her hand and started running. "Come on!" he shouted. "We need to take cover." A bolt of lightning flashed, and all the lights in town went dark.

The kids stumbled to the nearest building. Peter yanked the door open. It was completely dark inside. He reached into his backpack for his flashlight. The floors creaked and groaned with each step. Piper wanted to go back outside. This old building was creepy!

Her clothes soaked to the skin, Piper's teeth began chattering. "Peter, I th-th-think I hear s-s-something!"

Peter heard it too, his heart pounding as they moved slowly toward the sound. Suddenly the flashlight went out.

Piper screamed. Peter held his hand against her mouth as they heard footsteps running toward them.

"I tell ye, Cap'n, I seen them two kids come in here!" a gruff voice said. The footsteps suddenly moved in the other direction.

"Whew, that was close," Peter whispered, moving deeper into the black hallway. He heard someone talking to him through it all...someone whispering, saying something he couldn't hear because of the howling wind. But as he listened desperately, he was sure that the voice was

his sister's and she was saying...

"PIRATES!"

The Mother Lode!

They were living his dream, and they were all alone in this dark, creepy place with no one to help them!

Peter spotted a door. A sliver of light shone under it. Twin cannons guarded the entrance. Peter spied a sign on the wall. When he read it, he burst out laughing. "We're in the Mel Fisher Maritime Heritage Society Museum!" he cried.

Peter slowly cracked open the door. As their eyes adjusted to the dim lighting, the children began to see treasure: gold doubloons, pieces of eight, and exquisite jewelry. A huge gold bar rested on a red velvet drape in a glass display case.

"Look, Peter," Piper whispered. "There's light under that door in the back."

The old wooden door creaked on its rusty hinges. Silently, the kids tiptoed into the room. They noticed a small, flickering candle on a desk. To their complete surprise, a young boy wearing a pirate hat and an eyepatch was perched on a stool behind it. He was writing something with

an old-fashioned quill pen. Peter squinted and then he saw it—a postcard!

Could this small boy be their pirate pen pal?

The boy suddenly looked up and saw Peter and Piper standing in the doorway. He looked startled for an instant and stopped writing. Then he smiled as if he had known them for years. "Ahoy, mateys!" he cried. "Me name's Jordan, and I'm glad ta see that ye finally made it to my door!"

Although the kids were surprised and excited to meet him, they were a little disappointed. They thought their pen pal was a real pirate.

Piper's eyes narrowed. This boy couldn't be more than eight years old. She wanted to bop him one after all they'd been through! She put her hands on her hips. "I thought you said you were a pirate!" she exclaimed.

"But I am!" the little boy insisted. He clomped out from behind the desk on a wooden peg leg, and shoved his too-big pirate hat up, taking the eyepatch with it. His blue eyes locked on Peter's and then he hung his head. "I lost me

86

The Mother Lode!

leg to cancer about six months ago," he explained, "but the doctor says I can go home soon."

Peter waited half a heartbeat to break into a wide smile. "Wow! I guess you really are a pirate!" he exclaimed.

Suddenly, Cap'n Slappy and Mr. Downey from the pirate show burst through the door with their swords drawn. Peter and Piper pushed Jordan behind them, ready to defend him.

Peter felt a tug on his shirt. "That's me dad," Jordan said proudly.

Cap'n Slappy laid down his sword with a clang. "I hope we didn't scare you," he said. "We weren't sure who was in here with Jordan."

Peter's face lit up. "You were the man in the parking lot when we arrived!" he said. "No wonder you said we'd met before when you talked to me during the pirate show!"

"Peter and Piper Post! Where are you?" A woman's voice **permeated** the air.

Peter looked at Jordan. "That would be me mom," he said with a wink.

88

The Mother Lode!

The kids brought Mom in to meet Jordan and his dad. A concerned parent immediately took the place of the pirate character. They spoke quietly while the kids got to know each other better in the other room.

"When Jordan finally had to lose his leg, I just didn't know what to tell him," Jordan's dad explained. "His mother and I thought he'd adjust better if he could pretend to be a pirate. We'd been reading pirate stories and he had been **intrigued** with eyepatches and the old wooden peg legs. I told him he'd be like the pirates in the stories. The rest of us have just been playing the game with him. He's been hanging out here at the museum while he recuperates. We'll be going home tomorrow."

"He's been through quite an ordeal," Mom observed. "I think you've helped him more than you realize with the gift of imagination."

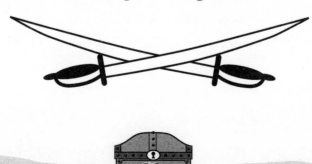

Dear Pirate: The Buried Treasure Mystery

Peter and Piper wanted to spend as much time with Jordan as they could. They talked for a while and admired his peg leg. Finally, Peter asked him, "We're curious about something. Your postcards spoke of the Mel Fisher treasure. We'd really like to see it. Do you know where it is?"

The boy grinned and crooked a finger at them. "Aye," he said. "Follow me. Do *I* have something to show *you*!"

With no hesitation at all, Peter and Piper followed him into the back of the Mel Fisher Maritime Heritage Society Museum.

The Mother Lode!

The End

Dear Pirate: The Buried Treasure Mystery

Postlogue

As the sun set over the water, the Post family prepared to set sail for home. Dad wanted to drive at night to avoid the traffic.

Peter leaned over the balcony of their room for a last glance at the spectacular sunset, and watched a magnificent, 80-foot yacht set sail. Her name stood out in gold against the whiteness of the ship: Atocha II.

On board, the crew was busy trimming the sails.

"Is the young prince comfortable?" the pirate with the gold teeth asked.

"Aye, I mean yes, Your Highness," Mr. Downey said with a bow.

The formal behavior of a royal family was back in place for the trip home.

"I want to set up college funds for Peter and Piper," the king said. "Those two children gave Prince Jordan something to live for and I shall never forget them."

Dear Pirate: The Buried Treasure Mystery

"As you wish, Sire," Mr. Downey said with a bow.

Mr. Downey yanked off his eyepatch. "Arrr, I be glad ta be rid of this thing," he said, tossing it over the side. "It itched terribly!" He and the king leaned on the rail and watched as it floated away.

"Ha! What are you crying about?" the king exclaimed. "I have to go to the dentist to get these gold caps removed!" They both laughed heartily. It was all worth it to help the young prince.

The cook came up from the galley to announce that dinner was served. "Ze Sparrow has also prepared the prince's favorite cake for dessert," he said.

Jordan, who was practicing tying rope knots nearby, was curious. "How do you know what my favorite cake is?" he asked.

The man smiled. "Why, Ze Sparrow, he knows all!" he said, and they all laughed.

94

About the Author

Carole Marsh is an author and publisher who has written many works of fiction and non-fiction for young readers. She travels throughout the United States and around the world to research her books. In 1979, Carole Marsh was named Communicator of the Year for her corporate communications work with major national and international corporations.

Marsh is the founder and CEO of Gallopade International, established in 1979. Today, Gallopade International is widely recognized as a leading source of educational materials for every state and many countries. Marsh and Gallopade were recipients of the 2004 Teachers' Choice Award. Marsh has written more than 50 Carole Marsh Mysteries™. In 2007, she was named Georgia Author of the Year. Years ago, her children, Michele and Michael, were the original characters in her mystery books. Today, they continue the Carole Marsh Books tradition by working at Gallopade. By adding grandchildren Grant and Christina as new mystery characters, she has continued the tradition for a third generation.

Ms. Marsh welcomes correspondence from her readers. You can e-mail her at fanclub@gallopade.com, visit the carolemarshmysteries.com website, or write to her in care of Gallopade International, P.O. Box 2779, Peachtree City, Georgia, 30269 USA.

A Pirate's Life for Me!

Ahoy! Me name is Jack, and I'm a pirate. How did I get here? Let me tell ye!

When I was but a lad of nine years, I had nowhere to live but in the streets of London. Me mum and dad died of the typhoid. I was an orphan. I spent me days in the streets looking for something to eat with me mates.

One day, we went to the docks. I heard that lads like me could get a job as a cabin boy on a ship. A cap'n there took a likin' to me, and asked me to join his crew. I was excited! Me—sailin' on the high seas!

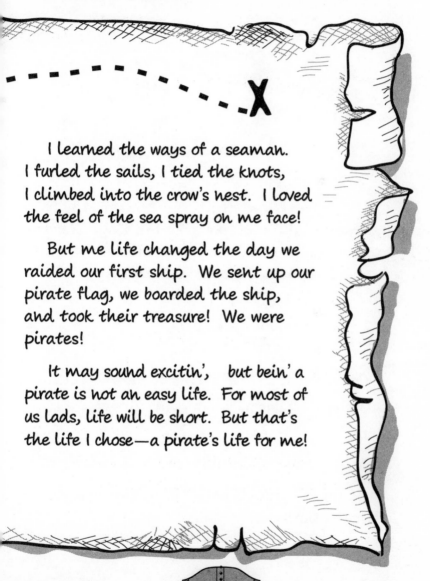

I learned the ways of a seaman. I furled the sails, I tied the knots, I climbed into the crow's nest. I loved the feel of the sea spray on me face!

But me life changed the day we raided our first ship. We sent up our pirate flag, we boarded the ship, and took their treasure! We were pirates!

It may sound excitin', but bein' a pirate is not an easy life. For most of us lads, life will be short. But that's the life I chose—a pirate's life for me!

Did you know that September 19 is International Talk Like a Pirate Day? Read on, and you'll be ready to participate!

The first thing you need to do is:

Say "ye" for you

Say "me" for my or mine

Say "Arrrrrr!" whenever you want!

Other great pirate terms to know:

Avast!: "Hey!" or "Stop that!" or "Who goes there?"

Aye!: "I agree!" or "Yes, sir!"

Beauty: "me beauty" is a nice way to address a lady

Talk like a Pirate!

Blimey!: an exclamation of surprise

Booty: loot, or treasure

Bucko: "me bucko" is "my friend"

Cap'n: short for "captain"

Davy Jones locker: the bottom of the sea

Hearties: a pirate captain might call his crew "me hearties"

Lad, lass, lassie: use to address someone younger than you

Landlubber: a non-sailor

Matey: use to address someone, like "Ahoy, matey!"

Shiver me timbers!: another exclamation of surprise

Walk the plank: pirate victim is forced to walk a plank into the water below

Wench: a female (but you might get better results by using the term "beauty")

Yo-ho-ho!: What pirates say!

About Pirates!

Frequently Asked Questions

1. What is a pirate?

A thief who robbed ships.

2. What were other names for pirates?

Corsairs or buccaneers.

3. What type of treasure did pirates want?

Treasure chests containing gold, silver, and jewels, plus things they needed, like food, barrels of wine, tools, and equipment for their ships like sails and anchors.

4. What is a Jolly Roger?

"Jolly Roger" is a generic term for a pirate flag. It is often used to describe the classic "skull and crossbones" pirate flag.

Most pirate captains and ships had their own special flag. They were usually made of ragged fabric spattered with paint. Besides being a rallying symbol—like our football

mascots of today—they were supposed to scare anyone who saw them.

5. Why did so many pirates sail in the Caribbean Sea?

They raided the Spanish galleons transporting valuable goods from the New World back to Europe. Pirates made so many raids that galleons began sailing together in fleets for protection.

6. Did anyone fight back against pirates?

In the 18th century, some countries decided they had to fight back against pirates. They sent their naval warships to battle them. Some famous pirates like Blackbeard were killed in these battles.

7. What was the Golden Age of Piracy?

A period of time from the 1680s to the 1720s where piracy grew throughout the Caribbean Sea, the American coast, the western coast of Africa, and the Indian Ocean.

Built-In Book Club

Talk About It!

1. Which character are you most like, Peter or Piper? Why?

2. If you were a pirate, what would be your signature look? An eyepatch and a peg leg, or a parrot named Polly who sits on your shoulder? Be creative!

3. Did the ending of this book surprise you? What did you expect to happen?

4. Do you have a brother or a sister? Do you get along with them? Discuss what it would be like to go on an adventure with your brother or sister.

5. Peter dreams of a living a pirate's life. Would you want to live a life of great adventure

on the open sea? Why or why not?

6. Peter and Piper are amazed by what The Sparrow tells them. Do you believe that fortune tellers can really read minds? Why or why not?

7. Peter asks Piper for help when he can't figure out the mystery of the postcards. When they work together, they solve the mystery quickly. Is it hard for you to ask for help sometimes, even when you really need it? Why?

8. At the beginning of the book, Peter has a nightmare about pirates. Later, he feels like he is experiencing déjà vu when things from his dream start happening in real life. Have you ever experienced déjà vu? If so, describe what it felt like.

9. What was your favorite part of the story?

10. Jordan imagines he's a pirate to take his mind off his illness. Sometimes imagining a different life for ourselves makes us feel better. Can you remember a time in your life when you used your imagination to make yourself feel better? Do you think Jordan's imagination made him happier?

Built-In Book Club

Bring It To Life!

1. Pen Pals! Have each book club member ask their mom or dad about a relative or family friend they haven't talked to in a while. Maybe it is a second cousin or an old friend from kindergarten. If you have a current address for that person, write a one-page letter to your new pen pal. You can tell them about yourself, your favorite vacation, your hobbies or your hidden talent—anything you want! Send the letter, and be sure to include your own address so your new pen pal can write you back!

2. Costume Contest! Have each member raid their closets at home to put together a pirate outfit. Be creative! Then, at your next meeting, have each member show up in their costume. Take pictures and ask a book club member's mom or dad to judge the contest. The best pirate wins!

3. Ahoy Matey! Write down as many pirate words you can think of and their meanings on one list. Make sure everyone contributes. After each member has seen the list, put it away. See how long you can hold a conversation using only pirate words. Ye best try yer hardest, or else ye'll walk the plank!

4. X marks the spot! Have each member find a map of their favorite state. Have everyone draw a small X on a city they'd like to visit. Then have them pass the maps to the person next to them and see if they can find the X. The person to spot the first X wins! After the group has found all the Xs, have each member explain why they would like to visit that city. What adventures await them there?

Pirate Trivia

1. Pirates used flags called "Jolly Rogers" on their ships to terrify their enemies. The flags often had pictures of skeletons, daggers or the infamous skull and crossbones.

2. Buccaneers were French settlers who lived on Caribbean islands when they got kicked off their pirate ship. Most buccaneers hunted wild boar and oxen!

3. Anne Bonny was a woman who disguised herself in men's clothes and snuck on board a pirate ship. She turned out to be one of the fiercest pirates to ever sail in the Caribbean!

4. Privateers and pirates are not the same thing. Privateers

carried a government license to pillage ships. Pirates did not.

5. Pirates who lost their hand in battle would often replace it with a metal hook because it was a useful tool around the ship. The hook would be held in place by long leather straps that wrapped around the pirate's shoulder.

6. A pirate had to sign a copy of The Articles before he could join the ship's crew. The Articles were a list of rules that every pirate had to follow.

7. Pirates really did have peg legs! Pirates were often hurt in battle and lost their legs. A substitute was required for their missing leg. So, they would look around their ship to find something that would work, like a long piece of wood.

8. Most pirates thought it was bad luck to have a woman aboard their ship!

Key West Trivia

1. Key West is farther south than any other city in the continental United States!

2. The Florida Keys are made up of about 1,700 small islands, but only 43 of them are connected by bridges!

3. Key West has the highest average temperature in the United States. It's a hot city!

4. Spanish explorers originally named Key West *Cayo Hueso* or "Bone Key." Legend says they found bones of dead Indians on the beach!

5. Many famous people like Ernest Hemingway, Truman Capote and Calvin Klein have lived in Key West!

6. In Key West, the locals are referred to as "conchs" because they live close to the water just like seashells!

7. Key West is a very tiny island. It is only four miles wide and two miles long!

8. Key West was the richest city in the United States in the late 1800s. The city got most of its money from pirates who raided the ships that had crashed on the coral reefs surrounding the island!

Glossary

 anxiety: a feeling of fear, nervousness or dread

 contagious: easily spread from one person to another

déjà vu: the feeling that you have experienced that moment before

exquisite: extremely beautiful, elegant or refined

galleon: a large, square-masted ship from the 1500s used for war and commerce

 intrigue: cause to be interested or curious

 maritime: involving ships, navigation, men of the sea, and the ocean

Glossary

navigate: managing the direction or course of something

 permeate: to spread or pass through something

pieces of eight: gold Spanish dollars that are no longer used

vague: not clearly understood or expressed

wench: an informal term for a young woman

S**cavenger Hunt

Want to have some fun? Let's go on a scavenger hunt! See if you can find the items below related to the mystery. (*Teachers: You have permission to reproduce this page for your students.*)

1. ___ A map of Florida

2. ___ A postcard

3. ___ Some rope (to tie sailor's knots with!)

4. ___ A picture of a sunset

5. ___ A pail and shovel (for digging up treasure!)

6. ___ A brightly colored bandana

7. ___ A black ink pen (for writing to your pen pal!)

8. ___ One fact about Mel Fisher

9. ___ A flashlight

10. ___ A pair of big gold hoop earrings (just like a pirate, matey!)

Pop Quiz

1. What city do Peter and Piper visit on their vacation?

2. True or False? The name of Peter's pen pal is Pirate Kiddy.

3. What is the name of the hotel where Peter and Piper stay?

4. True or False? Peter thinks his pen pal is a real pirate.

5. What scares Piper about The Sparrow's hands?

6. Where do Peter and Piper find their mysterious pen pal?

7. Who is Cap'n Slappy?

8. What is Captain Kid's real name?

113

TECH CONNECTS

Hey, Kids!
Visit www.carolemarshmysteries.com to:

• Join the Carole Marsh Mysteries Fan Club!

• Write one sensational sentence using all five
SAT words in the glossary!

• Play a Pirate Trivia Game!

• Read Frequently Asked Questions about
pirates!

• Learn about famous pirates—male and
female!

• Download a Scavenger Hunt!

• And much more!